Eyes Can Talk

LANA JEAN MITCHELL
Illustrations by Gilbert Young

To order additional copies of this book, contact:
Xlibris
1-888-795-4274
www.Xlibris.com
Orders@Xlibris.com

ISBN: 978-1-9845-8641-4 (sc)
ISBN: 978-1-9845-8642-1 (hc)
ISBN: 978-1-9845-8640-7 (e)

Library of Congress Control Number: 2020912447

Print information available on the last page

Rev. date: 07/15/2020

Eyes Can Talk

Two Funny, Funny, Short, Short Stories and a Bridge

By

Lana Jean Mitchell

Table of Contents

Dedication

This book is dedicated to Samory Palmer, Samory A. Monds,
Demarion Palmer, Tekeno Palmer, Shadea Palmer, Devon
Palmer, Angela Palmer, Elliott F. Monds, and Edith Calimese.

Acknowledgements

Eyes Can Talk!!! Would not be this
enjoyable book, without the

persons who helped me. Elliott F. Monds, and Samory
Palmer read the book and gave it their thumps up.

Thanks Xlibris Publishers

Introduction

Eyes Can Talk! is a children's book for children six to eight years old. *Eyes Can Talk!* is about some of the ways eyes talk. It is about some of the things eyes say.

In this book, eyes talk in two funny, funny, short, short stories and a narrative. *The ABC's of Reading* is one of the short, shorts. In the story, four-year-old Chikere (Che-KEH-reh) has eyes that say "We might need glasses!" to her pre-school teacher.

In *Little Is Sleepy*, the other short-short, three-year-old Little's drowsy eyes open and close like a jack-in-the-box to say "He is sleepy."

Remember when you were Little's age and didn't like going to bed? Little doesn't want to go to bed, no matter what his eyes are telling his grandmother. LOL (Laugh Out Loud).

You might know other things eyes can say. The talking eyes in this book don't say everything that eyes can say. Have fun looking at eyes. Look at your eyes, your friends' eyes, the teacher's eyes, all eyes, and see other things eyes can say.

See the eyes smile.

The funny, funny, short, shorts, are connected by a bridge.

The bridge is a narrative that has other things human eyes say, and a teeny, tiny bit of information about the eyes of birds of prey.

How about that—it rhymes!

A left lens, the first story, a right lens, the second story, and a bridge equals glasses so talking eyes can see.

The ABC's of Reading
(One funny, funny, short, short story)

A friend of a friend, my friend's "FOAF," tells the story of his preschool-age daughter, Chikere (Che-KEH-reh) L. Loveher, whose pre-school teacher, Mr. T. Talker, said to her dad, "Mr. L. Loveher, Chikere needs her eyes examined. Her eyes are saying she might need glasses."

8

So, with loving concern, Mr. L. Loveher takes his baby daughter to Dr. Daniel H. Hale, MD, the family doctor. As Dr. Daniel H. Hale prepares to test the pretty ebony child, he asks, "Chikere, can you read?"

"No," Chikere replies immediately.
Turning to Mr. L. Loveher, who is standing close by, Dr. Daniel H. Hale says, "Mr. L. Loveher, I cannot test Chikere."

And he gives him the name of another doctor, Dr. Mary C. Sight, a children's eye specialist.

A few days later, Chikere and her dad are in Dr. Mary C. Sight's office. Chikere is once again being prepared for an eye exam.

"Do you know your ABC's?" quizzes Dr. Mary C. Sight.

9

"Yes!" bright-eyed Chikere answers, and happily begins singing the letters of the alphabet as proof.

A B C D E F G

H I J K L M N O P

Q R S

T U V

W X Y and Z

Surprised and angry, thinking about the additional time off from work and the additional money spent on Dr. Mary C. Sight, Mr. L. Loveher asks harshly, "Chikere Loveher! Why did you tell Dr. Daniel H. Hale you couldn't read?"

"I can't read," Chikere says, startled and visibly shaken by her father's angry tone.

"But you just told Dr. Mary C. Sight you could!" Mr. L. Loveher says, pointing to the smiling Dr. Mary C. Sight and growing angrier by the second.

"No! I didn't!" Chikere Loveher says, as tears drop from her eyes. "Dr. Daniel H. Hale asked if I could read. I can't read. But I do know my ABC's. " Chikere Loveher, says, looking from her father's irate face to Dr. Mary C. Sight. And in a slow, soft, and trembling voice she begins again to sing the ABC's.

A B C D E F G

H I J K L M N O P

Q R S

T U V

W X Y and Z

Meeting eyes, Dr. Mary C. Sight and Mr. L. Loveher explode with laughter.

Mr. L. Loveher bends and kisses the center of his baby girl's head and says, "Now I remember. You first learn to sing the ABC's song, and then you learn to read the words."

Dr. Mary C. Sight completes the eye exam, and Chikere Loveher and her father order a pair of blue-framed glasses.

Chikere says to her father, "The glasses are sure to help me read the big rhyming book at preschool. I can see the pictures better."

T. Talker, Chikere's teacher, sees her glasses and says, "Chikere your glasses are very pretty," as he passes her the big rhyming book, her favorite book.

THE END

The eye chart that a doctor uses to test eyes was developed by Dr. Hermann Snellen. Dr. Snellen created the eye chart in the 1960s.

The eye chart has eleven rows of alphabetical letters. The top row of the eye chart contains one large letter. Sometimes the letter is a big *E*. But other letters can be used, such as *N* or *C* or *H* or *A* or other letters of the alphabet.

The other ten rows contain letters that get smaller and smaller, like NCHA, NCHA, NCHA, descending in size.

Human eyes can read a letter sharply from a distance of five feet. But we cannot see as sharply as birds of prey. Birds of prey, such as eagles and hawks, can see an animal from farther away. The eagle can see an animal sharply about twenty feet away.

Birds are more different from us than any other class of creatures. Birds can see polarized and ultraviolet light, and they experience colors we can never know.

When you cannot read sharply from a distance of five feet, your eyes might be saying "We need glasses!"

They, your eyes, can also say "We are 20/20 healthy, we have 20/20 vision."

"The eye is l a a a z z z y y y!" an eye might say to a doctor, or "I need a pirate's patch."

"We cannot see," the eyes might say, or "We are crossed."

"We are light sensitive," say eyes, or "I am a pink eye."

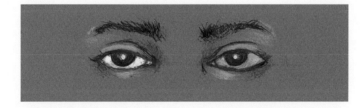

We have binocular vision, like an owl," the eyes can say when examined.

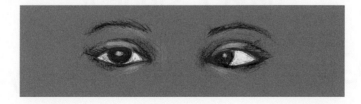

"We squint to read when we concentrate on school work,"

"We close when we are tired."

Tired / Sleepy?

Guess who else is sleepy!

Little Is Sleepy

(Second funny, funny, short, short story)

Little is our grandson.

His name is Marcus.

Little has the first name of his father, Marcus.

Little's father is B-I-G Marcus.

His son is called LITTLE!

Little is three and a half years old.

It is the hour of his bedtime.

He is watching his favorite cartoon.

His eyes close and then pop open like a jack-in-the-box.

Little looks around to see if we, saw his eyes open and close.

I am Little's grandmother.

"It's bedtime, Little!" I say.

"I'm not sleepy," says Little.

"Your eyes say you're sleepy," I say and smile.

"Eyes can't talk!" says Little.

"Eyes can talk, and yours say you're sleepy," I say.

Little covers his eyes with his hands as if to say, maybe my eyes do say I'm sleepy.

I turn to hide my smile.

"Can you see my eyes now?" he slurs drowsily, like a music box whose crank needs another turn.

Laugh out loud, I think.

"No," I say. "But your words sound funny."

Little removes his hands from his eyes. "I don't want to go to bed," he says. "I'm not sleepy."

"Little is in denial, I think."

21

"He is denying that he is sleepy, he's denying that it is bedtime and he's denying that he can't keep his eyes open."

"Your eyes say you're sleepy," I say again.

Little covers his eyes with his hands again. "Can you see my eyes now?" he asks again.

"No," I say and laugh out loud. I take Little's hand and walk towards the stairs.

I remember another night he wasn't sleepy and fell asleep on the landing at the top of the stairs.

HaHaHa!

He slept there for an hour before I woke him up and got him ready for bed.

"Let's choose tomorrow's clothes," I say.

"Let's brush our teeth,"

"Let's give you a bath,"

"Let's read bedtime stories,"

"Let's put you to bed."

"Say good night to Granddad," I say.

"Good night, Granddad," says Little.

"Good night, Little," says Granddad.

"Kisses mean love," says Little to Granddad.

"Kisses mean love," says Granddad back to Little.

He gives Little a BIG good-night kiss.

Little kisses and hugs Granddad good night.

And a yawning Little and I go up the stairs.

THE END

Resources/References

Hellem, Amy, and Gary Heiting. "Visual Acuity: Is '20/20' Perfect Vision?"All About Vision, updated April 2019. https://www.allaboutvision.com/eye-exam/2020-vision.htm

Allaboutvision.com. Liz Segre, reviewed by Gary Heiting, OD Eye Testing—The Eye Chart and 20/20 Vision. goggle.com

Montgomery, Sy. *Birdology: Adventures with Hip Hop Parrots, Cantankerous Cassowaries, Crabby Crows, Peripatetic Pigeons, Hens, Hawks, and Hummingbirds.* New York: Free Press, 2010. 3–5

Webmd.com

Welcome to webmd Eye tv

Wolchover, Natalie. "What If Humans Had Eagle Vision?" February 24, 2012 https://www.livescience.com/18658-humans-eagle-vision.html.

Printed in the United States
By Bookmasters